Sparty's Journey Through The Great Lakes State

Aimee Aryal

Illustrated by Cheri Nowak

MASCOT BOOKS

www.mascotbooks.com

Opened in 1923, Spartan Stadium holds 75,000 spectators for MSU football games.

The Spartan statue was introduced in 1943.

Sparty was enjoying a relaxing summer on the campus of Michigan State University. With football season fast approaching, Sparty decided to take one last summer vacation. He thought it would be fun to take a journey throughout the Great Lakes State, where he could see many interesting places and make new friends along the way.

Sparty packed his bags and left his home inside Spartan Stadium. He admired the famous Sparty statue near the stadium before making his way to Beaumont Tower.

MSU's most recognized campus landmark, Beaumont Tower, stands 105 feet tall and was completed in 1928.

Before leaving campus, Sparty ran into some of his friends. "Goodbye, Sparty! Have a nice trip!" said Michigan State fans. The mascot hopped in the Sparty Mobile and was on his way!

MSU's Abrams Planetarium

MSU's Kresge Art Museum

Sparty's first two stops were right on Michigan State's campus. At the Abrams Planetarium, Sparty met a MSU scientist who taught him interesting facts about our planet and solar system. He was impressed by Sparty's curiosity. The scientist said, "Go, State!"

Sparty's next stop was Michigan State's Kresge Art Museum, where the mascot admired art from around the world.

The Michigan State Capitol was completed in 1878.

After leaving Michigan State's beautiful campus, Sparty drove over to Lansing. Sparty knew that Lansing was the capital of Michigan and he was excited to learn more about the state's government. The mascot ran into a young Spartan fan on the capitol grounds. The fan cheered, "Hello, Sparty!"

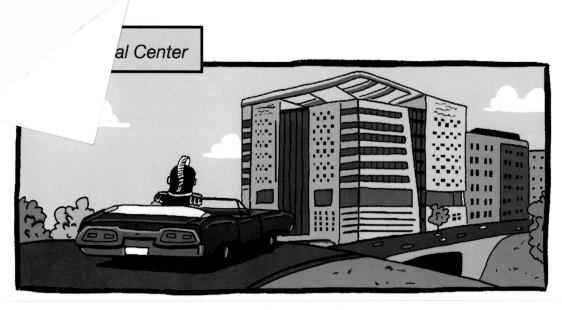

al Center

Sparty traveled west to Grand Rapids, where he made a stop at the new MSU Medical Center. Sparty had fun visiting with patients and the medical staff. The doctors reminded Sparty to exercise often and to always eat his vegetables.

Sparty's next stop was the historic Grand Rapids Library, where he checked out several of his favorite books. Sparty loved to read, especially books about mascots and Michigan State.

Grand Rapids Library

Gerald R. Ford Presidential Library and Museum

Sparty continued to the Gerald R. Ford Presidential Library and Museum, where he learned about the only Michiganian to become President of the United States.

Sparty toured the exhibits with great interest, but his favorite part of the tour was sitting behind the desk in the replica Oval Office. Sparty imagined himself as President!

Sparty continued west to Grand Haven Beach along Lake Michigan. Sparty was excited to relax and soak up the Michigan sunshine. As he lounged on a beach chair, he noticed a group of children playing nearby.

The children asked the mascot to help them build a sandcastle, but Sparty had another idea! He showed the children how to make a model of another important structure - Spartan Stadium. The children cheered, "Go, State!"

Michigan's West Coast boasts some of the best beaches in the Great Lakes region.

The lighthouse on South Manitou Island was built in 1871.

Sparty continued north along Lake Michigan to South Manitou Island. He had heard all about the lighthouse on the island, so he stopped there first. At the lighthouse, he ran into a young Spartan fan. Overhead, a flock of seagulls spotted the mascot and squawked, "Hello, Sparty!"

Staying on South Manitou Island, Sparty checked out Sleeping Bear Dunes National Lakeshore. He toured the dunes with MSU alumni. The alumni sure were happy to see Sparty again!

From the dunes, Sparty decided to water ski back to Michigan's west coast. The boat's driver called, "Go, Sparty, go!"

Sleeping Bear Dunes National Lakeshore is located near Traverse City along the northwest coast of Michigan's Lower Peninsula.

The Mackinac Bridge connects Michigan's Lower Peninsula with Michigan's Upper Peninsula.

Sparty drove north all the way to Michigan's Upper Peninsula. To get there, he had to drive the Sparty Mobile across Mackinac Bridge.

The mascot marveled at the scenic beauty the U.P. had to offer. At Tahquamenon Falls, Sparty spent the day with "Yoopers" from the Upper Peninsula. The Yoopers said, "Welcome to the U.P., Sparty!"

Because of its brown waters, Tahquamenon Falls has been nicknamed "Root Beer Falls."

After a full day of exploring Michigan's great outdoors, Sparty and his new friends set up camp in the wilderness. The group gathered around a campfire to roast s'mores and swap stories. "Go, Green! Go, White!" chanted his friends.

Mackinac Island is located on the eastern end of the Straights of Mackinac on Lake Huron.

Next, it was on to Mackinac Island by way of the Mackinac Ferry. During the ferry ride, the mascot and his friends enjoyed spectacular views of Lake Huron, Lake Michigan, and the Straits of Mackinac.

Sparty toured Mackinac Island on his bicycle. Everywhere the mascot peddled, his fans recognized him. "Hello, Sparty! Welcome to Mackinac Island!" said residents of the island.

That evening, Sparty checked in to the luxurious Grand Hotel. The mascot was greeted by Michigan State fans upon his arrival. They cheered, "Hello, Sparty! Go, State!"

Opened in 1887, the historic Grand Hotel on Mackinac Island claims to have the world's largest porch.

From Mackinac Island, Sparty drove south. After spending so much time in the Sparty Mobile, the mascot was ready to get sporty! He grabbed his fishing rod and headed out on Saginaw Bay. In no time, the mascot hooked a big one! In a worried voice, the fish said, "Hello, Sparty!"

Saginaw Bay is a favorite destination for walleye fisherman.

Next, Sparty traded his boots for a pair of ice skates. Sparty amazed the locals with his skating and puck handling skills. "Skate on, Sparty!" said a hockey player.

Finally, Sparty hit the links for a round of golf. On the eighteenth hole, he sunk an incredible putt to win the golf tournament. His playing partner said, "Nice birdie putt, Sparty!"

With over 800 golf courses, Michigan is a popular golfing destination.

The Detroit Zoo is home to nearly 8,000 animals.

Sparty's next stop was Michigan's largest city, Detroit. There was so much to do in Detroit!

At the Detroit Zoo, Sparty toured the animal exhibits and learned about each animal's habitat. He visited lions, tigers, elephants, and he even stopped to see a wolverine. Sparty didn't care much for the wolverine!

From the zoo, Sparty went to Hart Plaza at the Detroit International Riverfront. He played in the water with other Michigan State fans. The fans called, "Hello, Sparty!"

At sunset, Sparty explored the Detroit River and enjoyed great views of the skyline. From the riverbanks, his fans yelled, "Hello, Sparty!"

The Detroit River connects Lake Saint Clair to Lake Erie.

"Hockeytown" is one of Detroit's nicknames.

That evening, Sparty attended a Red Wings hockey game. After a score, a hockey fan yelled, "Goal, Sparty!"

Between periods, fans were surprised to see Sparty driving the Zamboni. As the mascot drove from one end of the rink to the other, hockey fans cheered, "Hello, Sparty!"

"Motown" is a style of music that originated in Detroit and is now one of the city's nicknames.

Sparty was ready to explore more of Detroit's culture and heritage. At the famous Fox Theatre, he posed for a picture with a Michigan State fan. "Say cheeeeese, Sparty!" said the fan.

Inside the theatre, Sparty enjoyed a fabulous concert. Sparty picked up a saxophone and joined the fun. He delighted the crowd with his musical skills. The audience roared, "Jam on, Sparty!"

As the center of America's automotive industry, Detroit is also known as the "Motor City."

While in the "Motor City," Sparty went to the Renaissance Center and inspected all the new car models in the showroom. He especially liked seeing the concept cars of the future. Michigan State fans said, "Check out the wheels, Sparty!"

Sparty wanted to learn more about cars. An engineer showed Sparty how cars are designed on the computer. Sparty designed a beautiful green and white sportscar!

After seeing how modern automobiles are made, Sparty went to the Henry Ford Museum to learn more about the history of the automotive industry. Sparty loved seeing the vintage Model T. "This car sure is a beauty, Sparty!" said a nearby Spartan fan.

The clock tower at the Henry Ford Museum is a replica of Independence Hall in Philadelphia.

Finally, Sparty made it back to East Lansing and his home at Michigan State University. Sparty took a moment to think about all the places he had visited and the many friends he made along the way.

As Sparty drifted off to sleep, he thought, "Go, State!"

Good night, Sparty.

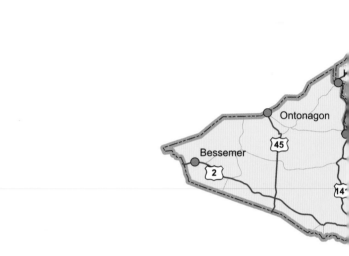

Sparty's Journey Through The Great Lakes State

For Anna and Maya. ~ Aimee Aryal

For "Homey B," my favorite Spartan! ~ Cheri Nowak

For more information about our products,
please visit us online at www.mascotbooks.com.

For more information, please contact Mascot Books,
P.O. Box 220157, Chantilly, VA 20153-0157

ISBN: 1-934878-30-8

Printed in the United States.

www.mascotbooks.com

Baseball

Boston Red Sox	Hello, *Wally*!	Jerry Remy
Boston Red Sox	*Wally The Green Monster And His Journey Through Red Sox Nation*!	Jerry Remy
Boston Red Sox	Coast to Coast with *Wally The Green Monster*	Jerry Remy
Boston Red Sox	A Season with *Wally The Green Monster*	Jerry Remy
Colorado Rockies	Hello, *Dinger*!	Aimee Aryal
Detroit Tigers	Hello, *Paws*!	Aimee Aryal
New York Yankees	Let's Go, *Yankees*!	Yogi Berra
New York Yankees	*Yankees Town*	Aimee Aryal
New York Mets	Hello, *Mr. Met*!	Rusty Staub
New York Mets	*Mr. Met* and his Journey Through the Big Apple	Aimee Aryal
St. Louis Cardinals	Hello, *Fredbird*!	Ozzie Smith
Philadelphia Phillies	Hello, *Phillie Phanatic*!	Aimee Aryal
Chicago Cubs	Let's Go, *Cubs*!	Aimee Aryal
Chicago White Sox	Let's Go, *White Sox*!	Aimee Aryal
Cleveland Indians	Hello, *Slider*!	Bob Feller
Seattle Mariners	Hello, *Mariner Moose*!	Aimee Aryal
Washington Nationals	Hello, *Screech*!	Aimee Aryal
Milwaukee Brewers	Hello, *Bernie Brewer*!	Aimee Aryal

College

Alabama	Hello, Big Al!	Aimee Aryal
Alabama	Roll Tide!	Ken Stabler
Alabama	Big Al's Journey Through the Yellowhammer State	Aimee Aryal
Arizona	Hello, Wilbur!	Lute Olson
Arizona State	Hello, Sparky!	Aimee Aryal
Arkansas	Hello, Big Red!	Aimee Aryal
Arkansas	Big Red's Journey Through the Razorback State	Aimee Aryal
Auburn	Hello, Aubie!	Aimee Aryal
Auburn	War Eagle!	Pat Dye
Auburn	Aubie's Journey Through the Yellowhammer State	Aimee Aryal
Boston College	Hello, Baldwin!	Aimee Aryal
Brigham Young	Hello, Cosmo!	LaVell Edwards
Cal - Berkeley	Hello, Oski!	Aimee Aryal
Clemson	Hello, Tiger!	Aimee Aryal
Clemson	Tiger's Journey Through the Palmetto State	Aimee Aryal
Colorado	Hello, Ralphie!	Aimee Aryal
Connecticut	Hello, Jonathan!	Aimee Aryal
Duke	Hello, Blue Devil!	Aimee Aryal
Florida	Hello, Albert!	Aimee Aryal
Florida	Albert's Journey Through the Sunshine State	Aimee Aryal
Florida State	Let's Go, 'Noles!	Aimee Aryal
Georgia	Hello, Hairy Dawg!	Aimee Aryal
Georgia	How 'Bout Them Dawgs!	Vince Dooley
Georgia	Hairy Dawg's Journey Through the Peach State	Vince Dooley
Georgia Tech	Hello, Buzz!	Aimee Aryal
Gonzaga	Spike, The Gonzaga Bulldog	Mike Pringle
Illinois	Let's Go, Illini!	Aimee Aryal
Indiana	Let's Go, Hoosiers!	Aimee Aryal
Iowa	Hello, Herky!	Aimee Aryal
Iowa State	Hello, Cy!	Amy DeLashmutt
James Madison	Hello, Duke Dog!	Aimee Aryal
Kansas	Hello, Big Jay!	Aimee Aryal
Kansas State	Hello, Willie!	Dan Walter
Kentucky	Hello, Wildcat!	Aimee Aryal
LSU	Hello, Mike!	Aimee Aryal
LSU	Mike's Journey Through the Bayou State	Aimee Aryal
Maryland	Hello, Testudo!	Aimee Aryal
Michigan	Let's Go, Blue!	Aimee Aryal
Michigan State	Hello, Sparty!	Aimee Aryal
Michigan State	Sparty's Journey Through Michigan	Aimee Aryal
Middle Tennessee	Hello, Lightning!	Aimee Aryal
Minnesota	Hello, Goldy!	Aimee Aryal
Mississippi	Hello, Colonel Rebel!	Aimee Aryal

Pro Football

Carolina Panthers	Let's Go, Panthers!	Aimee Aryal
Chicago Bears	Let's Go, Bears!	Aimee Aryal
Dallas Cowboys	How 'Bout Them Cowboys!	Aimee Aryal
Green Bay Packers	Go, Pack, Go!	Aimee Aryal
Kansas City Chiefs	Let's Go, Chiefs!	Aimee Aryal
Minnesota Vikings	Let's Go, Vikings!	Aimee Aryal
New York Giants	Let's Go, Giants!	Aimee Aryal
New York Jets	J-E-T-S! Jets, Jets, Jets!	Aimee Aryal
New England Patriots	Let's Go, Patriots!	Aimee Aryal
Pittsburg Steelers	Here We Go, Steelers!	Aimee Aryal
Seattle Seahawks	Let's Go, Seahawks!	Aimee Aryal
Washington Redskins	Hail To The Redskins!	Aimee Aryal

Basketball

Dallas Mavericks	Let's Go, Mavs!	Mark Cuban
Boston Celtics	Let's Go, Celtics!	Aimee Aryal

Other

Kentucky Derby	White Diamond Runs For The Roses	Aimee Aryal
Marine Corps Marathon	Run, Miles, Run!	Aimee Aryal
Mississippi State	Hello, Bully!	Aimee Aryal
Missouri	Hello, Truman!	Todd Donoho
Missouri	Hello, Truman! Show Me Missouri!	Todd Donoho
Nebraska	Hello, Herbie Husker!	Aimee Aryal
North Carolina	Hello, Rameses!	Aimee Aryal
North Carolina	Rameses' Journey Through the Tar Heel State	Aimee Aryal
North Carolina St.	Hello, Mr. Wuf!	Aimee Aryal
North Carolina St.	Mr. Wuf's Journey Through North Carolina	Aimee Aryal
Northern Arizona	Hello, Louie!	Jeanette S. Baker
Notre Dame	Let's Go, Irish!	Aimee Aryal
Ohio State	Hello, Brutus!	Aimee Aryal
Ohio State	Brutus' Journey	Aimee Aryal
Oklahoma	Let's Go, Sooners!	Aimee Aryal
Oklahoma State	Hello, Pistol Pete!	Aimee Aryal
Oregon	Go Ducks!	Aimee Aryal
Oregon State	Hello, Benny the Beaver!	Aimee Aryal
Penn State	Hello, Nittany Lion!	Aimee Aryal
Penn State	We Are Penn State!	Joe Paterno
Purdue	Hello, Purdue Pete!	Aimee Aryal
Rutgers	Hello, Scarlet Knight!	Aimee Aryal
South Carolina	Hello, Cocky!	Aimee Aryal
South Carolina	Cocky's Journey Through the Palmetto State	Aimee Aryal
So. California	Hello, Tommy Trojan!	Aimee Aryal
Syracuse	Hello, Otto!	Aimee Aryal
Tennessee	Hello, Smokey!	Aimee Aryal
Tennessee	Smokey's Journey Through the Volunteer State	Aimee Aryal
Texas	Hello, Hook 'Em!	Aimee Aryal
Texas	Hook 'Em's Journey Through the Lone Star State	Aimee Aryal
Texas A & M	Howdy, Reveille!	Aimee Aryal
Texas A & M	Reveille's Journey Through the Lone Star State	Aimee Aryal
Texas Tech	Hello, Masked Rider!	Aimee Aryal
UCLA	Hello, Joe Bruin!	Aimee Aryal
Virginia	Hello, CavMan!	Aimee Aryal
Virginia Tech	Hello, Hokie Bird!	Aimee Aryal
Virginia Tech	Yea, It's Hokie Game Day!	Frank Beamer
Virginia Tech	Hokie Bird's Journey Through Virginia	Aimee Aryal
Wake Forest	Hello, Demon Deacon!	Aimee Aryal
Washington	Hello, Harry the Husky!	Aimee Aryal
Washington State	Hello, Butch!	Aimee Aryal
West Virginia	Hello, Mountaineer!	Aimee Aryal
West Virginia	The Mountaineer's Journey Through West Virginia	Leslie H. Haning
Wisconsin	Hello, Bucky!	Aimee Aryal
Wisconsin	Bucky's Journey Through the Badger State	Aimee Aryal

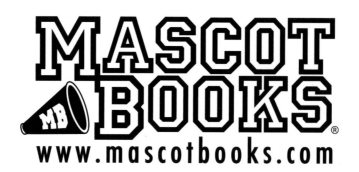
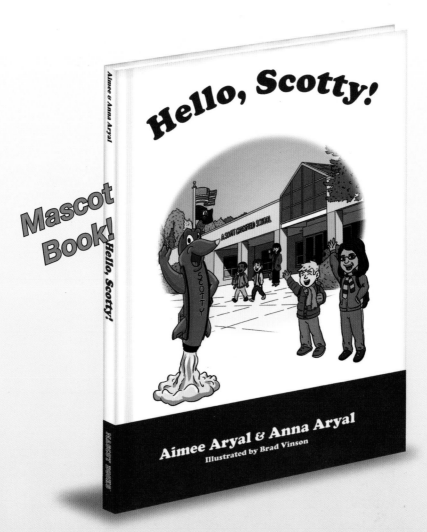